The Three Little Astronauts

There are lots of Early Reader
stories you might enjoy.

Look at the back of the book,
or for a complete list, visit
www.orionchildrensbooks.co.uk

The Three Little Astronauts

SKY HAWK

GEORGIE ADAMS

ILLUSTRATED BY EMILY BOLAM

Orion
Children's Books

ORION CHILDREN'S BOOKS

First published in Great Britain in 2016
by Hodder and Stoughton

1 3 5 7 9 10 8 6 4 2

Text © Georgie Adams, 2016
Illustrations © Emily Bolam, 2016

The moral rights of the author and illustrator have been asserted.

A CIP catalogue record for this book
is available from the British Library.

ISBN 978 1 4440 1626 0

Printed and bound in China

The paper and board used in this book are from well-managed forests
and other responsible sources.

Orion Children's Books
An imprint of
Hachette Children's Group
Part of Hodder and Stoughton
Carmelite House
50 Victoria Embankment
London EC4Y 0DZ

An Hachette UK Company
www.hachette.co.uk

www.hachettechildrens.co.uk

For Jenna Aldridge – GA

Contents

Chapter 1

Meet the Astronauts!

"Hello! We're the Three Little Astronauts, calling from Outer Space."

"Hi! I'm Rikki. Welcome aboard our space ship Sky Hawk."

"I'm Jenna. It's our job to keep order around the universe."

"I'm Leo. We're always prepared for trouble!"

"This is our robot friend, Pal."

"Come with us. We'll show you around."

"Here's the galley where we eat. Everything floats around in space, so we heat up food in cook bags."

"If we didn't, chips, baked beans and tomato sauce would fly all over the place!"

"Our favourite snacks are Astro-nuts. They taste yummy! But they're hard to find and we don't have many left."

"This is where we sleep. We snuggle into
sleeping pods and close the lids, to keep us
safe inside."

"These are the booster rockets. At Astronaut School we learn how space ships work. So we know how to repair Sky Hawk if anything goes wrong with the engine."

"And here is the flight deck. We can climb
a ladder to the look-out to see the stars —"

One morning, a warning light flashed on the control panel. An urgent voice came through a speaker:

"Mission Control to Sky Hawk! Can you hear me?"

"Yes, Mission Control, we can hear you," said Rikki.

"We've received a signal from Bod who lives on the Pink Planet. Bod has seen a rocket ship, Dark Star, flying around. He thinks it's going to attack!"

"Uh oh!" said Rikki. "Dark Star belongs to that no good villain, Zarl. Sounds like he's up to his tricks again."

"The Pink Planet?" said Jenna. "That's where Astro-nuts grow. You won't find them anywhere else in the whole universe! Maybe that's why Zarl is there?"

"Leave it to us, Mission Control." said Leo. "We're on our way. Over and out."

Chapter 2

Rikki Takes a Wrong Turn

The universe is big. Very BIG. The little astronauts asked robot Pal where to find the Pink Planet.

Pal looked confused.

"Pink-plant?" he said very slowly.

"I don't know where to find a pink plant."

"Oh no," groaned Jenna. "Pal's battery has run down. He's talking rubbish. What now?"

"We'll look for the planet on my star map!"
said Leo.

"There are millions and millions of stars,"
said Rikki. "It could be anywhere!"

Jenna was the first to spot it.
"There!" she cried.

PINK
PLANET

The three little astronauts jumped into action.

"My turn to be pilot," said Rikki, taking
the control stick.

"I'll read the map," said Jenna.

"I'll fire the booster rockets," said Leo. "It's my favourite job! Stand by for blast-off."

"FIVE,
FOUR,
THREE,
TWO,
ONE —"
WHOOOOOOSH!

Sky Hawk zoomed away at top speed. Soon they were flying close to the Milky Way.

Jenna checked the map.
"Turn left, Rikki. Now!"

But Rikki had caught sight of something strange through his window, and was wondering what it was. Instead of turning left, he pushed the control stick to the right.

Sky Hawk whizzed through the Milky Way
and out the other side.

"Where are we?" said Jenna.

"Sorry!" said Rikki. "I think I took a
wrong turn."

Then the others saw what Rikki had spotted
earlier. Only now it was nearer. It was a hole
in the sky.

The biggest, darkest hole they'd ever seen.

Chapter 3

Spinning Through Space

The Black Hole pulled Sky Hawk towards it. There was nothing the little astronauts could do.

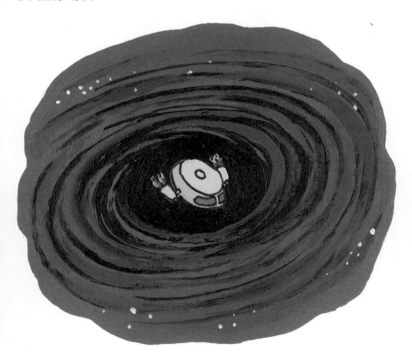

The space ship spun round and round, like a sock in a washing-machine. Rikki, Jenna and Leo tumbled through time and space, until —

Sky Hawk suddenly shot from the Black
Hole.

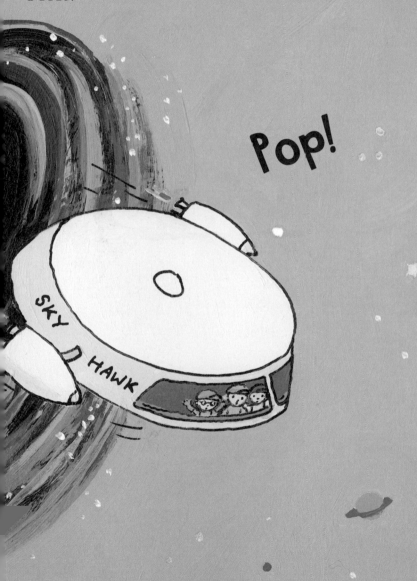

Pop!

"Ooo!" said Rikki, holding his head.
"I feel dizzy," said Jenna.
"I feel sick," said Leo.

But Robot Pal was smiling.
"My battery has re-charged!" he said.

Then, just as the three little astronauts were starting to recover, Pal said:

"WE ARE APPROACHING PLANET EARTH. PREPARE TO LAND!"

Chapter 4

The Last Dinosaur

Sky Hawk landed with a thud! Rikki, Jenna and Leo opened the hatch door and ran down the steps to check for damage. Apart from one small dent, their space ship was okay.

"Phew!" said Leo. "We were lucky."

He jumped in the air and fell on his
bottom. Bump!
"Ouch!" he said. "I forgot I wasn't floating
in space."

"Earth has gravity." said Rikki.
"It keeps everything on the ground –
including you!"

"Get up, Leo," said Jenna. "We can't stay here. We're on an important mission. We must find the Pink Planet."

It was then they saw the monster.

"D-d-d-dinosaur!" they said nervously.

"But it can't be!" said Rikki. "Dinosaurs lived on Earth millions of years ago."

"So why is this one here?" said Leo.

"I think we've travelled back in time!" Jenna said. "It must have happened when we fell through the Black Hole."

"This is all my fault," Rikki said. "If only I'd turned left at the Milky Way."

The dinosaur came closer.

"Run!" said Rikki.

"Hide!" said Jenna.

"Wait!" said Leo.

To their surprise, they saw tears rolling down the dinosaur's cheek.

"W-w-what's the matter?" said Leo.

"I'm Daisy," said the dinosaur. "All my friends have gone. I'm the last dinosaur left on Earth. I'm very lonely."

The little astronauts felt sorry for Daisy.
"What can we do?" said Jenna.
"Can I come with you?" said Daisy. "Please!"

The little astronauts wanted to help.
"We can't leave her," said Leo.
Everyone agreed.
"Yes, Daisy. You can come with us!"

Daisy waved her tail to show how happy she was — swish, swish, swish!

Then they all squeezed into Sky Hawk and headed for the Pink Planet.

Chapter 5
The Pink Planet

It was Jenna's turn to take the controls. They flew fast through space until, at last, they saw the glow of the Pink Planet ahead.

Jenna landed Sky Hawk behind a tall rock
and the little astronauts got out. They
walked around the rock to the other side . . .

"Oh no!" said Rikki.

"I was right," said Jenna angrily. "Look! Zarl is taking away loads of Astro-nuts!"

"We must stop him," said Leo.

Just then, a boy came running up. He was very pleased to see the little astronauts.

"Thank the stars you're here!" he said. "I'm Bod. We're in big trouble! Zarl is collecting all the Astro-nuts for himself."

"We can't let him get away with this!" said
Rikki. He marched off to see Zarl, but his
tummy felt wobbly. Zarl and his gang were
an ugly bunch of villains.

"Wait for us!" said Jenna and Leo, running
after him.

When Zarl saw the three little astronauts he sneered and shouted orders to his gang:

"Grab the little troublemakers! Set them to work! I'll make lots of money selling Astro-nuts. And no one is going to stop me!"

At that very moment, Daisy the dinosaur
walked out from behind the rock.
Zarl had never seen anything so scary.

"I didn't know there were monsters about,"
Zarl cried. "Run for it, men. Run!"

They raced to their rocket ship and flew
away as fast they could.

Everyone cheered.
"Good riddance!" said Bod.

"I don't think Zarl will be back," said Leo.
"Not with a monster about!" said Jenna.

They all looked at Daisy, she had discovered
an Astro-nut tree.
"Mmm! These nuts are delicious!" she said
happily. "Can I stay here, please?"
And everyone said:
"Yes!"

So Daisy stayed on the Pink Planet with her
new friends and was never lonely again.

Bod thanked Rikki, Jenna and Leo for coming to their rescue, and gave them each a big bag of Astro-nuts.

Soon it was time for the little astronauts to be on their way.

So now we must leave them and say:

"Goodbye, Rikki."

"Goodbye, Jenna."

"Goodbye, Leo."

"Goodbye, little astronauts.
Goodbye!"

What are you going to read next?

Don't miss the other adventures
in the **Three Little series**...

Have a spooky
Halloween with the
Three Little Vampires.

Go on a magical
adventure with the
Three Little Magicians.

If you like The Three Little Astronauts, you'll also enjoy **Algy's Amazing Adventures in Space**,

or learn all about the universe with a **non-fiction Early Reader**.